SOMEWHERE,
NOT SO FAR AWAY,
there's a cave on a hill,
filled with wonderful creatures.

You could be nearer to it than you think.
Look down . . . Is that a tiny
winding path? Are they stripy mounds
beside a sparkling sea? If there are lights
at the cave windows, and you can hear
excited chatter, look closer.

You may have found the home of the

little
SOMETHINGS

To Ella and Oliver Marchant

and Sandra Glare and Richard Bentley

J.L.

To Lal and Jill

A.P.

EGMONT

We bring stories to life

First published in Great Britain 2014
by Egmont UK Limited
The Yellow Building, 1 Nicholas Road, London W11 4AN
www.egmont.co.uk

Text copyright © Jill Lewis 2014
Illustrations copyright © Ali Pye 2014

The moral rights of the author and illustrator have been asserted

ISBN 978 1 4052 6819 6

A CIP catalogue record for this title is available from the British Library

SOMETHING MISSING

Jill Lewis ✳ Ali Pye

EGMONT

In the cave on the hill
the Little Somethings were getting
ready for Trippety Doodah Day.

As usual, they were having a picnic by the sea
with the Big Somethings. But this year it was
extra exciting because they were going to ride
to the beach on Trunky's scooter . . .

. . . as soon as he had made a few changes.

Outside the cave, Trunky had collected bits and bobs,
handles and knobs, sprockets and screws,
and hammer and glue.

"I'll soon have this sorted and then
we'll be ready to go," he smiled.

But back in the cave,
Bob wasn't ready to go.
"We're missing a Little Something –
I must tell Trunky!" he said.

Everyone looked at everyone else.
Who was missing?

Trunky was bursting with pride when Bob ran out. "Look at this," he said, showing Bob the extra long platform with cushioned seats.

"Very nice," said Bob,
"but we're not ready yet!
A Little Something is missing!"
and with that he was gone.

Trunky walked round the scooter scratching his head. What was missing?

"Of course! A **sail**. Silly me," he said, hauling and heaving a roll of cloth from the pile.

Back inside the cave,
everyone was looking for
the missing Little Something.

"Listen up!" called Bob, 'I've checked the passenger list and the missing Something is . . .

Little Hogwash. We have to find him!"

Everyone scattered and started looking in tiny spaces and hidden places.

Bob ✓   Bumpkins ✓
Spike Fox ✓   Crackle ✓
Skidadder ✓   Quiff ✓
Miniwiggler ✓   Twiglittle ✓
Little Hogwash   Sparky ✓
Star ✓   Trunky ✓
Snaggles ✓
Stingle ✓
Spring Chicken ✓

"I'd better tell Trunky that a Little Something is still missing," said Bob.

Trunky was resting on the picnic
basket when Bob bustled out again.
"Hey, Bob! It's ready to go.
Take a look at this," said Trunky,
pointing at the sail.

"Well done," replied Bob hurriedly, "but we can't go yet,
a Little Something is still **missing** and it's …"

"Really?" interrupted Trunky, surprised.

"YES, REALLY!" cried
Bob and he dashed back
into the cave.

"Hmm," thought Trunky,
"maybe he's right." He headed
back to the pile of bits and bobs.

"Of course," he muttered, spotting the
frying pan. "We'll need pancakes, silly me,"
and he wiggled and jiggled it out of the pile.

Soon, there was nowhere left to look inside the cave, so all the worried Little Somethings rushed outside to search.

"I'm ready!" shouted Trunky, picking up the picnic basket.
"It's Trippety Time!"

No one moved.

"All aboard!" Trunky shouted.

But still no one moved.

Bob stepped forward.
"Trunky, I've told you already,
a Little Something's **missing** and . . ."

"Hang on," Trunky replied crossly.
"It's got a **sail**, a **frying pan**, and I've
even remembered the **picnic basket**.
I've thought of everything!"

"The scooter's great, Trunky,"
Bob explained, "BUT there is still
a Little Something missing . . .

and that something is Little Hogwash!"

Missing

Trunky was so surprised that he dropped the picnic basket.
It landed with a thump and the lid flew open.

"Ouch," a voice said

and out tumbled . . .

"Little Hogwash!" everyone cheered.

"What were you doing in there?" asked Trunky.

"I just needed a little something to eat
before we set off," yawned Little Hogwash,
"and then I had a nap."

"So at last we've got everyone
and everything . . .
ALL ABOARD!" called Trunky.

Trunky stood on the scooter and tried to push off.

Oh! Nothing happened.

He tried again.

The scooter didn't move.

"Is something **missing**?" asked Bob.

"The wind's missing," said Trunky sadly.
"I hadn't thought of that."

No one knew what to do.

Just then, a Big Something came up the hill.
"What's the hold up?" asked Hoovle.
"The others are waiting down by the sea."

Trunky pointed to the sail hanging down and shook his head sadly.

Hoovle chuckled. "Don't worry, there's a little something I can do to help."
He took a deep breath.

1, 2, 3 . . . and he **hoovled**
for all he was worth.
The sail filled and the scooter
sped down the hill.

It was a wonderful day at the seaside – with something for everyone and at last not a single thing missing.

One Little Something
is taking the picture.
Can you work out
who it is?

A SPOTTER GUIDE TO THE
little SOMETHINGS

Spike Fox

Bob

Little Hogwash

Skidaddler

Miniwiggler

Snaggles

Quiff

Star

Twiglittle

Sparky

Stingle

Crackle

Bunnikins

Trunky

Spring Chicken